THE ZACK FILES™

The Misfortune Cookie

For Judith, and for the real Zack,
with love—D.G.

THE ZACK FILES™

The Misfortune Cookie

By Dan Greenburg

Illustrated by Jack E. Davis

SCHOLASTIC INC.

New York Toronto London Auckland Sydney
Mexico City New Delhi Hong Kong

I'd like to thank my editors,
Jane O'Connor and Judy Donnelly,
who make the process of writing and revising
so much fun, and without whom
these books would not exist.

I also want to thank
Jennifer Dussling and Laura Driscoll
for their terrific ideas.

ISBN 0-439-28550-X

12 11 10 9 8 7 6 5 4 3 2   1 2 3 4 5 6/0

Printed in the U.S.A.   40

First Scholastic printing, March 2001

Chapter 1

Listen, I don't want to scare you or anything. But the next time you order Chinese food, watch out. Something very spooky might happen to you. I don't mean Chinese food itself is spooky. It's what comes with it. Fortune cookies.

I should know. I have had my share of weird fortunes in fortune cookies. But then lots of weird things are always happening to me. Once I was put under the curse of a Hawaiian volcano goddess. Another time I turned invisible after I drank some disappearing ink. In fact, weird things happen to me so much that by now I expect them.

Oh, I should tell you who I am and all that stuff. My name is Zack. I'm in the fifth grade at the Horace Hyde-White School for Boys in New York City.

The time I want to tell you about, my dad took me to a brand-new Chinese restaurant in his neighborhood. My parents are divorced. And I spend about half of every week at Dad's apartment.

The name of the restaurant was Wun Dum Guy. It really was. I'm not kidding you. You can believe me or not. It probably means something different in Chinese.

Most Chinese restaurants I've been to look about the same. They're really bright and noisy.

Wun Dum Guy was different. It was very dark, for one thing. And there were little jack-o'-lanterns on every table with candles inside them. There was a giant poster of the Easter Bunny on the wall, with a fuzzy white tail. There was a fish tank draped with Christmas tree lights. There were Hanukkah menorahs with heart-shaped candles in them. The only light came from the pumpkin candles, the Christmas tree lights, and the menorahs. It was very, very quiet.

One reason it was quiet was that Dad and I were the only customers in the place. I felt kind of sorry for the owners of Wun Dum Guy. Maybe the name had something to do with it.

We were sitting at a little table near the tank of fish. There were electric-blue fish and shiny green ones. There were orange-and-white-striped ones with spiky things sticking out all over the place. I hoped these guys weren't on the menu.

Soon a waiter came over to take our order. He didn't look like most Chinese waiters I've seen. He had a little beard, a ponytail, and three staples in his left ear.

"So, dudes," he said. "Can I, like, take your orders?"

"Yes," said Dad. "We'll have one order of chow fun noodles, please. And the moo shu chicken. And one order of fried rice."

I really like moo shu chicken, even though it sounds like something cows wear on their feet.

"Excellent," said the waiter. "Our moo shu is totally awesome, dudes. Would you like chopsticks?"

"Sure," said Dad.

The waiter gave us two sets of them. I'm not too good at eating with chopsticks. But I do like to fool around with them.

While we were waiting for our food, I played with my chopsticks. They make excellent drumsticks. I also told Dad all about this big baseball game we were going to play after school the next day. My school, Horace Hyde-White, was playing the Butch Quagmire School. They are these real jerks. I mean it. Well, I don't know if everybody in the whole Butch Quagmire School is a jerk. But the guys on their baseball team are. That's for sure. They act like they're too good to play us. Which they aren't.

I'm a third baseman, by the way. The coach thinks I'm not too bad. I mean, I almost never drop the ball. I'm not a power hitter or anything. But I usually get on base. And I can run like crazy.

By the time the waiter came back with the food, I'd stopped drumming with my chopsticks. I was now pretending they were fangs. Dad asked me to please stop and start eating. So I did.

The food was really great. Especially the

moo shu chicken. But there was about three times as much as anybody could eat. Anybody but Godzilla, I mean. Actually, even Godzilla would've had trouble finishing the chow fun noodles.

Dessert was two fortune cookies. Dad and I opened them and read our fortunes.

"Well, what does yours say?" Dad asked.

"You first," I said.

"Mine says, **'Tomorrow much money will come your way,'**" Dad answered with a big smile. "Now tell me yours."

"**'To win big, lose first,'**" I answered. I hate fortunes like that. I wanted one like Dad got. "Dad, what does that mean?"

"I don't know," he said. "**'To win big, lose first.'** Hmmm. Maybe it has something to do with dieting or something."

"Maybe," I said. "But that wouldn't have anything to do with me. I'm skinny."

Dad shrugged.

"You know," said Dad, "fortune cookies are just like newspaper horoscopes, Zack. You can read whatever you like into them."

I started fooling around with all the chopsticks again. By the time the waiter came by with the check, I had arranged three of them in the shape of a pyramid. Then I balanced the fourth one on the tip. When the waiter saw what I'd done, he looked amazed.

"Oh, wow," he said softly as he put the check on the table. "Like, that is totally outstanding, dude. Like, that means you are in perfect balance this week. I think maybe you're going to have, like, a very interesting week."

He smiled at us. A mysterious smile.

Now what could he mean by that?

Chapter 2

The next afternoon was our baseball game. The guys on the Butch Quagmire team were even bigger jerks than usual. Every time Spencer Sharp came up to bat, they made fun of the way he was standing.

"Hey, kid!" they yelled. "You getting ready to lay an egg?"

Spencer is the smartest kid in my class, and he's my best friend. But he does have a weird batting stance. He places his feet really far apart. And he squats down really low. I hate to say it. I could see what the

Quagmire kids meant about laying an egg.

It wasn't only Spencer who got picked on. They also made fun of other guys on our team. Like this kid in my class, Andrew Clancy, who's really tall.

"Hey, kid!" they yelled. "You better put flashing red lights on your head. Otherwise airplanes are going to crash into you!"

They also argued every close call the umpire made. They were a much better team than us. Still, we were playing really well. By the bottom of the ninth, the score was tied, 7 to 7. Our team was up. There was one out. It was my turn at bat. Vernon Manteuffel was on third. Vernon is *not* my friend. He's always telling you how rich his parents are. He also sweats a lot. He was probably sweating all over third base right now.

I stepped up to the plate. I really wanted to hit that ball as hard as I could. But I knew

I should I bunt it instead. Then I could prob-ably score Vernon from third. And if we got another run, that was it for the Quagmire team.

The first pitch was right over the plate. I knew what I had to do. I laid down a bunt and raced for first. I ran as hard as I could. Vernon took off for home like a rocket. For a blubber boy he sure could run. The pitch-er scooped up the ball and threw it to first. I was out, but Vernon scored. Those Butch Quagmire guys never knew what hit them! We won the game!

Everybody on the team crowded around me. Kids were slapping me on the back and giving me high fives, low fives, and medi-um-level fives. Even Vernon.

"That was smart playing," the coach told me. I really felt great.

Spencer and I kept going over the game all the way back to my dad's apartment.

Spencer was staying for dinner that night. Dad didn't feel like cooking, so we decided to order take-out Chinese food from Wun Dum Guy. We told Dad all about the game and how I bunted.

"That was really smart of you, Zack," he said. "To go for the bunt instead of the hit. It just shows you. Sometimes you have to give up something in order to gain something larger."

Hmmm. That was true. I was thrown out at first, but we won the game.

All of a sudden, it was like a light bulb snapping on in my head.

"Or, to put it another way," I said, "'**To win big, lose first.**'" I turned to Spencer. "That was the fortune inside my fortune cookie last night. So maybe it came true."

"Maybe," said Spencer.

"But mine said, '**Tomorrow much money will come your way,**'" said Dad.

Then he looked at his watch. "It's already seven-thirty. So time is running out."

Just then the doorbell rang. It was the food delivery. There was moo goo gai pan, egg foo yung, and my favorite—moo shu chicken. It all smelled great.

"Hey, Spencer," I said when I was finished eating. "Watch this."

I showed him my trick with the balancing chopsticks. Both he and Dad tried to do it. But their chopsticks kept falling down all over the place.

"I guess I must be the only one who's in balance this week," I said.

"What?" said Spencer.

Then I told him what the waiter had said.

"So I'm going to have a very interesting week," I said. "Whatever *that* means."

"Well, let's see what's in store for *all* of us," said Dad. He passed out a fortune cookie to each of us. Dad opened his first.

"Mine says, **'You will go on a long trip,'**" he said. "I wonder if that's where much money will come my way."

Spencer's fortune said, **"Your job will take you to Hong Kong, where you will have many children."**

"I can't handle more than two," said Spencer.

"What does yours say, Zack?" Dad asked.

"**'Sweet is the reward for those who pass the test of time,'**" I read. "Now this makes absolutely no sense," I said.

Oh, how wrong I was about that!

~~~

By the next morning I had forgotten all about the fortune in my fortune cookie. It turned out I had also forgotten there was going to be a quiz in Current Events.

Mr. Gatkes held up a copy of a newsmagazine with a picture of some guy's face on the cover.

"Why is this man on the cover of this magazine?" he asked. "Zack, do you know?"

I didn't have a clue.

"Uh, isn't that the guy who made the *Guinness Book of World Records* for continuous belching?" I said.

Everybody laughed.

"No," said Mr. Gatkes. I noticed he was not laughing.

Andrew Clancy raised his hand.

"Yes, Andrew?"

"Isn't that the guy who went for a whole year without changing his underwear?" said Andrew.

Everybody laughed again, but Andrew was just trying to top me.

"OK, class," said Mr. Gatkes. "Take out pencils and paper. Write down who this man is and why he's on the cover of the magazine."

Everybody wrote something and gave it to Mr. Gatkes, including Andrew and me. Mr. Gatkes looked over the papers.

"All right," he said. "Everybody but Zack and Andrew knew who it was. Vernon, stand up and tell the class whose picture is on the cover of the magazine."

"It's a scientist named Dr. Henry Schmutz," said Vernon, sweating. "He just won some big prize. He invented a tractor engine that uses cow pies for fuel."

"Thank you, Vernon," said Mr. Gatkes. "Everybody who knew the answer will go for ice cream at Len and Larry's after school today. Zack and Andrew, you'll have to stay in school an extra hour. And I want both of you to write me a report on Dr. Henry Schmutz. It is due next Monday."

Andrew and I groaned.

"I want a real report," said Mr. Gatkes.

"With illustrations and everything. You can start while we're at Len and Larry's."

Andrew and I groaned some more.

When the rest of the class left to get ice cream, Andrew and I jumped on the magazine and read all about Dr. Schmutz.

"Using cow pies for tractor fuel," I said. "What kind of a mind would come up with something like that?"

"Yeah," said Andrew. "What'll he think of next—using dog poop to run cars?"

"I actually wouldn't mind meeting somebody as weird as that," I said.

"Me either," said Andrew. "But I'm sure not lending him our Honda."

I had to laugh at that one.

We started writing our reports. It was hard. I kept thinking of Spencer and the rest of my friends at Len and Larry's, eating all that ice cream. What a sweet deal they'd gotten, just for knowing that guy on the cover of... I took a good look at the cover of the magazine. It was *Time*.

Boing! I felt almost as if a hammer had hit me over the head. **"Sweet is the reward for those who pass the test of time."** Ice cream was the sweet reward. And knowing about the guy on the cover of *Time* was the test. The fortune cookie had predicted this! Just like the other one predicted how I had to lose before our team won the baseball game.

There was something very spooky going on here. And I had to get to the bottom of it.

Chapter 3

As soon as the extra study period was over, I went to Len and Larry's Ice-Cream Parlor. I got there just as Spencer came out. He was licking his lips.

"What flavor did you have?" I asked.

"Cashew Cashew Gesundheit," he said.

That was the flavor we invented. The one that won the Len and Larry's Create-an-Ice-Cream-Flavor Contest not so long ago. But that's another story. Right now I had other things on my mind.

"So, Spencer," I said mysteriously. "I bet that ice cream was a *sweet reward*."

Spencer looked at me blankly.

"You know, for passing the test of *Time*," I hinted.

At first Spencer still looked blank. Then his eyes got wide and his mouth formed a perfect O.

"Oh, wow, Zack," he said. "*Time* magazine. That quiz in Gatkes's class was just like your fortune last night!"

I nodded.

"Spencer," I said. "I don't know how, but those Chinese fortune cookies are predicting things that are really happening to me. I'm going to try and find out why. You want to help?"

"I'm in," Spencer said.

I figured the best place to look for an answer was at Wun Dum Guy. So we took the bus there. It was between lunch and dinner, so the restaurant was empty. Although, come to think of it, the place was just as empty when Dad and I were there for dinner.

The waiter with the beard, the ponytail, and the staples in his ear came up to us. He seemed really glad to see us.

"Greetings, young gentlemen dudes!" he said. "You want a table?"

"No, no," I said. "We just came to ask you some questions."

He seemed kind of sad that we hadn't come to eat dinner.

"Like, what do you little dudes want to ask about?"

"Those fortune cookies you gave us," I said. "They came true for me."

He nodded.

"Fortune cookies tell fortunes, dudes," he said. "Like, why do you think they're called *fortune* cookies?"

"But they never came true before," I said. "And they didn't come true for my dad or my friend here."

The waiter shrugged.

"Like, maybe you've never been in balance before," he said.

This was really starting to creep me out. I didn't really like knowing stuff before it happened. So far none of the fortunes had been bad ones. But what if I got a scary one? Like one that said I was going to have to wear braces till I was thirty-four or something?

"Who writes the fortunes they put inside those cookies?" I asked.

"A special fortune cookie writer, dude," said the waiter.

"And where would we find this special fortune cookie writer?" Spencer asked.

"Ask Grandma Guy," said the waiter.

"And who is Grandma Guy?" I asked.

"Oh, like, Grandma Guy is a very special

woman, dude. Very wise, very wise. Very old, very special."

"And where would we find her?" Spencer asked.

"Wun Fat Sun Bakery," said the waiter. "In Chinatown."

Maybe this Grandma Guy could tell me what was going on. Chinatown. I had been there with Dad lots of times. But I'd never gone alone.

"Hey, Spencer," I said. "Do you think we should go down to Chinatown?"

"Sure. It won't take us long," he said. "We'll both be home before dinner."

We took the subway down to Chinatown. I love Chinatown. When you get out of the subway, it's like you aren't in New York anymore. It's like you're not even in the United States. That's how different it seems. It's like you've taken a Number 6 subway straight through the center of the earth to

China. Which would take a long time, because the Number 6 isn't even the express.

The streets in Chinatown are very narrow. The newsstands sell Chinese newspapers. The signs on the stores are in Chinese. The telephone booths have little Chinese pagoda tops on them. It's very cool.

Spencer and I went past a store selling dead ducks hanging upside down in the front window. There were dead octopuses with long, yucky-looking tentacles outside other stores. There were huge dead fish. There were pigs' heads. There were bowls full of fish eyes. People actually ate this stuff!

"I can't believe people actually eat this stuff," I whispered to Spencer.

"They probably can't believe you and I eat what we eat either," said Spencer.

"What do you mean?"

"Like hot dogs, for example," he said.

"Ground-up pigs' and horses' ears and feet and intestines."

"I see what you mean," I said.

We finally found the Wun Fat Sun Bakery. They had all kinds of little buns and cakes in the window. They looked pretty good, after what we saw in the other shops.

We went inside.

A tall, fat man wearing a white baker's hat stood behind a tiny counter. I figured he was the one fat son.

"Yes?" he said without smiling.

"We've come to see Grandma Guy," I told him.

He frowned at me. Had I said something wrong?

"Grandma Guy?" he repeated.

"Yes."

"There's no Grandma Guy here."

"Isn't this the Wun Fat Sun Bakery?" Spencer asked.

"Maybe," said the fat son.

"Well, we'd like to see Grandma Guy," said Spencer. "She works here."

"What makes you think somebody by the name of Grandma Guy works here?"

"The waiter at Wun Dum Guy told us," I said.

The fat son thought about this a moment. Then he nodded, and pointed over his shoulder.

"In there," he said. "Through those curtains."

We went around the counter and through the curtains. They were made of lots of long strands of beads.

The room we'd walked into was very dark. At first we couldn't see a thing. Then our eyes got used to the dim light.

At a little table sat an old Chinese woman. A very old woman. With a very wrinkled face. She looked two hundred years old,

easy. On the table was a heart-shaped candle in a little clay jack-o'-lantern. The very old woman was dressed in bell bottoms, a tie-dyed purple T-shirt, and a Pittsburgh Steelers jacket. There were two empty chairs at the table.

"Please come in, honorable young gentlemen," she said in this high, singsong voice. "Please sit down."

Spencer and I sat down on the two chairs.

"You must be Grandma Guy," I said.

"Why must I?" she asked.

"Well, are you?" Spencer said.

"Maybe yes," she said, "maybe no."

"Well, ma'am, which is it?" I asked.

"Mainly yes," she said.

"Glad to meet you, Grandma Guy," I said. "My name is Zack. And this is my friend Spencer. We came to ask you some questions about fortune cookies."

"What honorable young gentlemen wish

Grandma Guy to tell them about fortune cookies?"

"First," said Spencer, "are you the person who writes the fortunes?"

"Maybe yes," she said, "maybe no."

"Well, which is it?" I asked.

"Mainly yes," she said. "Grandma Guy is writer for many years. Very beloved writer. Grandma Guy's sayings are most beloved in the whole world."

"Can you give us some examples?" said Spencer.

"Oh, **'A penny saved is a penny put away somewhere safe.'**"

"I think the actual saying is, **'A penny saved is a penny *earned*,'**" said Spencer. "And Ben Franklin was the one who wrote that."

"Ben Franklin steal it from Grandma Guy in rough draft," she said. "Same with **'Early to bed and early to rise makes a** man smart, rich, and not sick much.' Grandma Guy try to sue Ben, but no lawyer would take the case."

"What are some of your others?" I asked.

"'A rolling stone gathers no earth-worms or centipedes.' 'An apple a day keeps the orthodontist away.' 'The squeaky wheel gets the sticky brown stuff.' And 'Don't look the gift horse in the nose.' Unfortunately, they not sell. Very hard to make living writing beloved say-ings."

"You actually knew Ben Franklin?" Spencer asked.

"Not well," said Grandma Guy. "Only to say hello at parties. Then he steal my beloved sayings. I tell him, Ben, go fly a kite. Because of Grandma Guy he discover electricity, but he get all the credit."

"Tell me," I said. "How do fortune cook-ies work? I mean, does every fortune find the person who's supposed to get it? Or does getting a certain fortune in a cookie make it happen to you?"

Grandma Guy smiled her mysterious smile, but she didn't answer. Instead she handed me four chopsticks.

"Build," she said. "Build pyramid."

I arranged three of them into a pyramid. I balanced the fourth one on the tip.

"Aha!" she said. "Just as Grandma thought. For this week, you lucky...or unlucky." Then she laughed a long time in a way I didn't like. "Fortune cookies only predict what lie ahead for *you*," she said. Then she pointed to me. "If you not wish to know what lie ahead, please not to read fortune cookies. You young gentlemen hungry?"

"Not really," said Spencer.

I remembered the great-looking Chinese pastries in the next room.

"*I'm* hungry," I said.

"You wish to order out pizza with pepperoni and anchovies?" she asked.

"Oh no, never mind," I said.

"Well," she said, getting up, "time for me to go. Grandma Guy must get to her other job."

"What's that?" asked Spencer.

"Weather girl on Channel 77, Chinese cable TV," she said. "But before I go, take fortune cookie." She handed me one. "Very tasty." Then she laughed again.

I didn't want to. But I took it.

"You wish to open?"

"Not really," I said.

"Fortunes never good for more than a few days," she said. "Then they turn sour, like milk you forget to put in icebox. This fortune good till Sunday. After Sunday, not work. But before Sunday, beware!"

Chapter 4

I went home. And for a whole forty-seven minutes I managed not to open the fortune cookie Grandma Guy had given me. This whole thing—the fortunes, being in balance—was turning into a full-blown weird thing. Just like all the other weird things that have happened to me. So I left the fortune cookie on Dad's kitchen table, right in its little plastic bag.

But then I got to figuring. My first fortune had turned out pretty well. It predicted I'd win the baseball game. The second one turned out OK too, at least for Spencer and the other guys. It said they'd get free ice cream at Len and Larry's. Maybe this next fortune was something great. Maybe I was going to be rich and famous. Maybe I was going to become third baseman for the New York Yankees.

I grabbed the little plastic bag and tore it open. I broke the cookie in half and read the fortune. It said, **"Beware! Danger lurks in lion's shadow."**

All the hairs on the back of my neck stood up. What the heck did *that* mean? Definitely not something good. Sometime this week was I going to run into a lion? And be chomped up like a kitty treat? How could that happen? I mean, let's face it. I live in New York, not Africa. No, I wasn't in any danger.

And yet...

And yet, until Sunday I was in perfect balance. Until Sunday all my fortunes would probably come true. Just like **"To win big, lose first."** Just like **"Sweet is the reward for those who pass the test of time."** Maybe the safest thing would be to avoid any place with any kind of lions. At least till after Sunday.

Suddenly, I heard something in the hallway outside my room. A creak in the floorboards. What the heck was it? Probably nothing. Probably just the usual noises a hallway makes when you're very quiet. Yeah, that's all it was.

But what if there was a lion outside my room?

No, that was crazy. How could a lion ever get into Dad's building? Get past the doorman? Walk into the lobby? Ride up in the elevator? Get out on the right floor? Find Dad's apartment? Get inside? No way. No way at all.

But what if there was a lion outside my room?

Now I heard it again. Heavy footsteps in the hallway right outside my room. Padding softly toward my door. Beads of sweat sprang out on my forehead and started rolling down my face. Sweat broke out on my back and under my arms. I was beginning to feel like Vernon Manteuffel.

The heavy footsteps stopped. Something pushed against my bedroom door. I watched the door creak slowly open. I held my breath. And then I saw what it was.

Chapter 5

It was Dad!

"Zack, guess what?" said Dad, coming into my room.

"What?"

"My editor at *Men's World* magazine gave me two free tickets to the New York Giants game on Sunday!"

"Awesome!" I said. "Who are they playing?"

"The Detroit Lions."

The Lions? Yikes!

"Dad, I'm afraid I can't go."

"Why not?"

"Because of Grandma Guy's warning."

"Who?"

"She's a lady we heard about at Wun Dum Guy. She writes fortunes for Chinese fortune cookies. Spencer and I met her at the Wun Fat Sun Bakery in Chinatown. She gave me this fortune."

I showed Dad the fortune.

"'**Beware! Danger lurks in lion's shadow,**'" Dad read. He frowned. "And this worries you?"

"Heck *yes*, it worries me," I said. "Grandma Guy has some really weird powers. Since I've been in balance, my fortunes have been coming true. I just don't want to take any chances, that's all."

"Well, I think you're overreacting," said Dad. "After all, *my* fortunes haven't come true—'**Tomorrow much money will come your way,**' and '**You will go on a long**

trip.' I think you're being really silly, Zack."

"Maybe," I said. "But you're not in balance like I am. So I'm just trying to avoid lions. At least this week, OK?"

Dad shrugged and went back to his study to work.

I hated to disappoint Dad. And I hated to miss the Giants game. But maybe the Lions were getting a real lion mascot. I wasn't too hot to have some crazy beast run up to me at halftime and chew my arm off. I don't know. Maybe I *was* overreacting.

The phone rang. Dad answered it.

"Zack, it's for you!" he called.

I picked up the phone in the kitchen.

"Hello," I said.

"Zack, it's Andrew."

"Hi, Andrew. What's up?"

"Zack, I'm calling to invite you to my birthday party. I hope you can come."

"Great," I said. "When is it?"

"This Friday after school," he said. "At the Bronx Zoo. We're meeting right outside the lion house."

The lion house! Yikes!

"Oh boy, Andrew," I said. "I'm afraid that's going to be a problem for me."

"You have something else to do on Friday?"

"Yeah, I'm afraid so," I said. "Actually, no. Frankly, Andrew, it's the lions that are the problem. See, the thing is...I happen to be really allergic to lions. The way some people are allergic to cats?"

"Really? What happens to you?"

"Uh, well, my face gets red and swells up like a balloon. And I break out in oozing zits all over the place. It's really gross. I mean, just looking at me would probably make you puke."

I might have overdone it. Sometimes

when I'm making up excuses, I get a little carried away.

"That's nothing," said Andrew. "If I drink grape juice, my skin turns purple. Then snot runs out of my nose, and I barf all over my clothes."

There he was, trying to top me again.

"Well, Zack," said Andrew, "it sounds like you probably shouldn't come to my party."

"Yeah, that's what I thought too. But thanks for asking me, Andrew."

"OK. Goodbye, Zack."

I couldn't believe all these lion things were suddenly coming into my life. I mean, you can go for a whole year without having to deal with lions. But then everybody in the world is throwing lion-based stuff at you.

About an hour later, the front doorbell rang.

"Dad!" I called out. "Somebody's at the door!"

"Can you see who it is?" Dad called back. "I'm right in the middle of something."

"OK," I said.

I went to the door and looked through the peephole. OK, OK, I admit it. I was afraid it might be a lion. There stood our next-door neighbor, Mrs. Taradash. She is definitely not one of my favorite people. But at least she isn't a lion. I opened the door.

"Hello, precious," she said.

She calls all kids "precious." But you can tell she doesn't think they are. She's complained to Dad a lot about me. That's because I do slam dunks on the backboard in my bedroom. She pretends to like me. But that's only because she has this big crush on Dad.

"Hi there, Mrs. Taradash," I said.

"I have a wonderful surprise for you, precious," she said.

"Yeah?" I said suspiciously. "What is it?"

"I've got three tickets for you, me, and your dad on Saturday night. Front-row seats at Madison Square Garden!"

"Really?" I said.

Hey, this might be good. For front-row tickets to see the New York Knicks I could even put up with Mrs. Taradash.

"Is it for a Knicks game?" I asked.

"No, precious," she said. "Much better than a Knicks game."

"What could be better than a Knicks game?" I asked.

"The Ringling Brothers, Barnum and Bailey Circus!"

Chapter 6

I thanked Mrs. Taradash politely and told her I couldn't go.

All the rest of the week I kept away from lions. I even made Dad change my dentist appointment with Dr. Lyons. I didn't read *The Lion, the Witch, and the Wardrobe,* which we were assigned in English. I wasn't taking any chances. If I could just get through Sunday, then the fortune would go sour. That's what Grandma Guy said.

When Sunday finally rolled around, I still hadn't finished my report on Dr. Henry

Schmutz, the cow pie guy. So I figured I'd spend the day doing that.

"Why don't we watch the Giants-Lions game on TV?" said Dad. "If any lions come to the door, we won't let them in."

"Hmmm." I thought that over. It was really tempting. "OK, why not?" I said.

I really did want to watch the Giants on TV. But then I started worrying. Maybe it was stupid to think a lion could reach me in Dad's apartment. But other bad things could happen if I watched the Lions on TV. I mean, the TV could blow up or something. Hey, it happens. I should know. It happened to me in a hotel room in Hawaii.

"On second thought, Dad," I said, "I'm going to skip it."

"Zack, you don't seriously think a lion could get into this apartment, do you?"

"Oh no," I said. "Not at all, not at all. Well, probably not."

"Then what's the problem?"

"Uh," I said, "I have this big report to do on Dr. Henry Schmutz. The guy who invented a tractor that uses cow pies for fuel? Anyway, it's due tomorrow. I better get to work."

"OK," said Dad.

So I went into my room and closed the door and finished my research. It turns out Dr. Schmutz is a pretty cool guy. Cow pies aren't the only thing he's fooled around with. He's also discovered a way to heat homes with chicken poop.

An hour later I was done with the report. But I realized I didn't have any poster board to tape my pictures to. I went into the living room, where Dad was watching the game.

"Dad, do you have any poster board?"

"No. Why?"

"Well, I need some for my report. Do you know any place we could buy some?"

"It's Sunday. Not many places are open.

I wish you'd thought of this yesterday."

"I really need it, Dad. I'm sorry I didn't remember till now."

"Come to think of it," he said, "there *is* one art supply place that's open on Sunday. It's on Fortieth Street and Fifth Avenue. If we hop in a cab right now, we can get there before it closes."

"Great!"

Traffic was awful because of some stupid parade further uptown. So Dad and I got out of the cab at Forty-first Street and Fifth. The sun was low in the sky, almost ready to set. The art supply store was just past the New York Public Library.

It was still sunny out, but when we passed in front of the library, we were suddenly swallowed up by this gigantic shadow. I looked up to see what was casting the shadow. And then I saw it.

A lion!

Chapter 7

I was standing right under one of the two huge stone lions who guard the steps at the Public Library!

Every warning light in my system flashed red and started buzzing. I totally panicked. I had to get out of there! I spun around so fast I tripped over my own feet. I fell and smacked my head on the bottom step. Fourth of July fireworks went off behind my eyes.

"Zack!" Dad shouted. "Are you OK?"

"Uh, I don't really know," I said. I sat up

and rubbed my head. Ouch! I was going to have a real bump there.

Dad looked me over. A little blood was trickling down my cheek. But outside of a small cut on my forehead, I seemed to be OK. Dad helped me to my feet. I dusted myself off. My head hurt, but suddenly I felt really relieved.

"Zack, why are you smiling?" Dad asked.

"Dad, don't you get it? **'Beware! Danger lurks in lion's shadow.'** This was what the fortune cookie was trying to warn me about. And trying to avoid it made it happen. But now I don't have to worry anymore."

"How do you feel?" he asked.

"Not too bad, really," I said. Then I smiled again. "You know, I'm really fine."

We got to the art supply store just before they closed and bought my poster board.

"Well, it looks as if your appointment with the lions is finally over," said Dad.

"Yes-s-s," I said, and punched the air with my fist. "I feel like this huge weight is off me."

"We ought to celebrate," said Dad.

"OK," I said.

"Are you in the mood for some Chinese food?"

I glared at Dad and shook my head.

"OK, OK. Then what about a movie?" he asked.

"Why not?" I said.

Dad bought a paper at the corner newsstand and looked up the movie schedules.

"Just to be on the safe side," I said, "maybe we ought to skip *The Lion King*."

We played it very safe. We went to see a movie about space warriors and giant cockroaches. There was zero chance of finding a single lion in it. Dad bought me a big bag of popcorn with lots of melted butter. That was my first mistake.

We settled into our seats. The theater got dark. The movie was about to start. I began stuffing my face with popcorn. That was my second mistake. In the middle of stuffing my face, I saw it. There, in the middle of the screen was...a lion! The MGM lion. It was roaring at me!

I shrieked, which was my third mistake. A bunch of unchewed popcorn went right down my throat. I choked. The movie screen got blurred and fuzzy.

"Zack, what's wrong?" Dad shouted.

I pointed at my throat. Dad started pounding on my back. He shouted for help. Things were getting fuzzier and darker. Ushers ran up to me. They were yelling things I could not understand. One of them grabbed me from behind. He started giving me the Heimlich maneuver.

And then I blacked out.

Chapter 8

I'm here to tell you that the Heimlich maneuver really works. If it didn't, I wouldn't be here to tell you anything at all.

To make up for my bad experience, the manager of the theater gave me fifty free tickets. Dad said maybe he was afraid we'd blame the popcorn and sue the theater or something. But I think he did it to be nice.

You won't believe this. But for dinner that night, I asked Dad to bring home some take-out from Wun Dum Guy. I felt different. A little off balance. I tried to make the chopsticks balance again. Just as I thought. No matter how hard I tried, I couldn't do it.

"I guess I'm finally out of balance," I said. "Which means the fortune cookies can't predict my future anymore."

"Thank heavens," said Dad.

To prove I had nothing to be scared of, I opened my fortune cookie. I read my fortune. It said, **"Tomorrow you will meet the one you'll marry."**

Dad and I had a big laugh over that. But the next morning, getting ready for school, I put on my favorite shirt and combed my hair with gel. Hey, you never know.

On the way to school, I passed Wun Dum Guy. But guess what? Wun Dum Guy was...gone! Completely gone! In its place was Pino's Popular Pizza Parlor.

I couldn't believe it. How could a restaurant disappear overnight? I was already a little late for school, but I had to find out what was going on. I went into Pino's Popular Pizza Parlor.

"Morning, young fella," said a guy in a white shirt and pants. "Want a slice?" He looked like he hadn't shaved in a couple of days.

"No," I said. "I'm looking for Wun Dum Guy."

Suddenly, he grabbed me by the front of my favorite shirt.

"Who are you calling a dumb guy?" he yelled.

"N-nobody!" I said. "That's the name of the restaurant that used to be here! Wun Dum Guy! It's a Chinese restaurant, I swear!"

He loosened his grip on the front of my favorite shirt.

"You sure that's no insult?"

"I swear!" I said. "Just please answer one question for me, OK?"

"OK," he said.

"There used to be a Chinese restaurant here. What happened to it?"

He looked at me like I was crazy. Then he shook his head.

"Kid, Pino's Popular Pizza Parlor has been right here for as long as I can remember," he said.

~~~~~~

I couldn't figure out what happened to Wun Dum Guy.

I asked around the neighborhood. Nobody could quite remember if there had ever been a Chinese restaurant on that block. Dad and I sure remember it, though. Spencer too.

Then last night, just before bedtime, I was flipping through the TV channels. As I went past Channel 77, I saw somebody I thought I recognized.

Standing in front of a big weather map.

Wearing a purple tie-dyed T-shirt and a Pittsburgh Steelers jacket.

It was Grandma Guy!

She was speaking Chinese, but on the screen they had what she was saying in English: "...RAINFALL WILL BE 44 INCHES, THE HIGH WILL BE 100°, AND THE LOW -7°. AND THAT IS THE WEATHER FOR THE NEXT TWELVE MONTHS. WHEN WE COME BACK I WILL GIVE YOU THE FIVE-YEAR FORECAST."